This book belongs to:

....

Based on the episode "Paddington's First Snow" by Toby Davies

Adapted by Lauren Holowaty

First published in Great Britain by
HarperCollins *Children's Books* in 2020
HarperCollins *Children's Books* is a division of HarperCollins*Publishers* Ltd,
HarperCollins Publishers
1 London Bridge Street
London SE1 9GF

The HarperCollins website address is:
www.harpercollins.co.uk

1 3 5 7 9 10 8 6 4 2

ISBN: 978-0-00-840730-8

Printed in Italy

Based on the Paddington novels written and created by Michael Bond

MIX
Paper from
responsible sources
FSC® C007454

FSC is a non-profit international organisation established to promote the
responsible management of the world's forests. Products carrying the FSC
label are independently certified to assure consumers that they come
from forests that are managed to meet the social, economic and
ecological needs of present and future generations.

Find out more about HarperCollins and the environment at
www.harpercollins.co.uk/green

The Adventures of Paddington™

First Snow

HarperCollins *Children's Books*

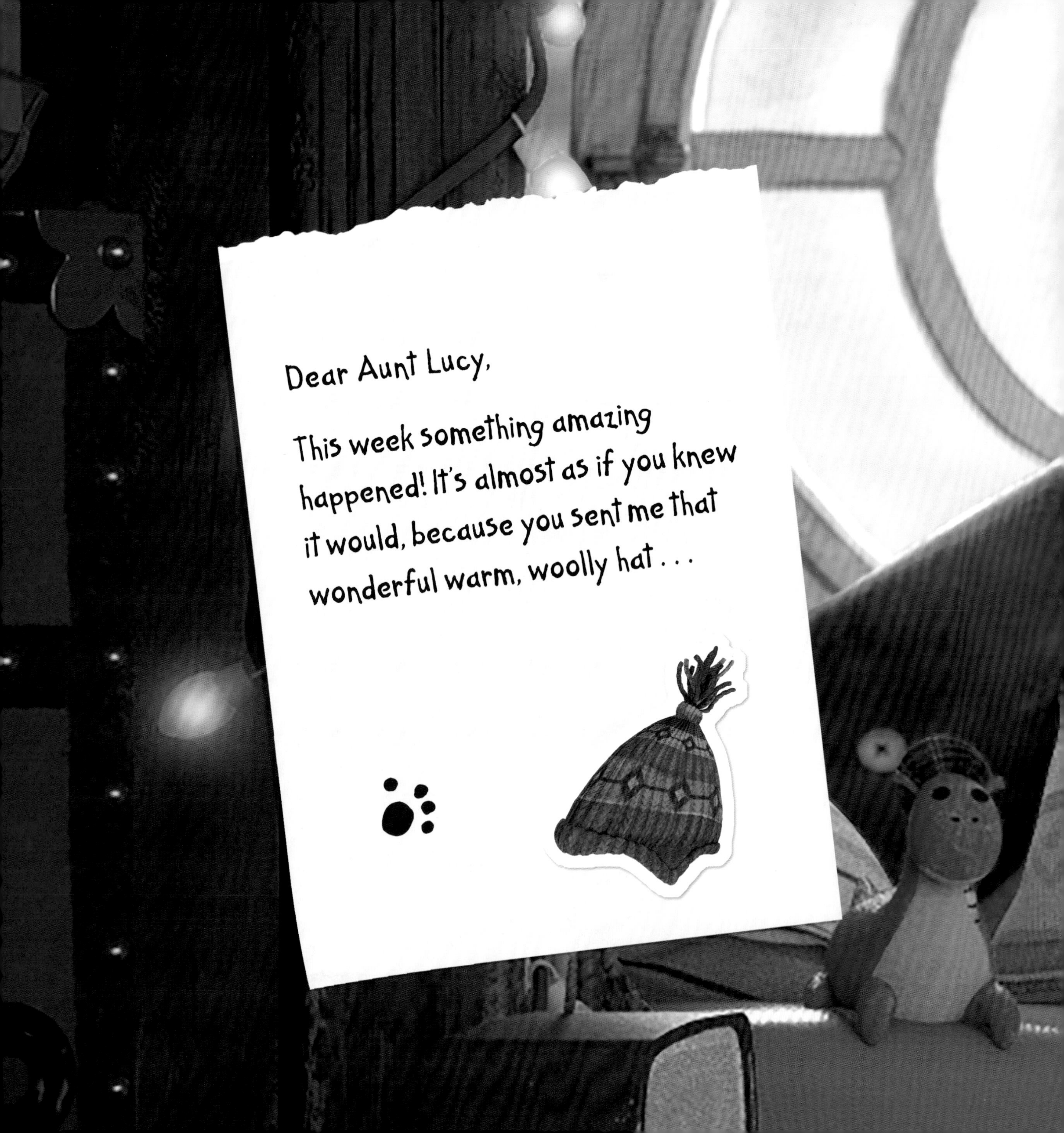

Dear Aunt Lucy,

This week something amazing happened! It's almost as if you knew it would, because you sent me that wonderful warm, woolly hat . . .

“After Captain Scott reached the South Pole, he began his dangerous journey home through the snow . . .” read Judy out loud.

“But did he *find* a yeti?” asked Jonathan.

“Of course not,” replied Judy. “They’re *not* real!”

"What's a yeti?" asked Paddington.

"It's a huge beast that lives in snow," growled Jonathan, pretending to be a yeti. "With great big claws and feet the size of . . ."

Paddington backed away nervously from Jonathan until . . .

. . . he fell on his bottom, knocking off his new woolly hat.

"Really big feet?" suggested Paddington.

"Exactly!" cried Jonathan.

"WHOOOAAA!"

Just then they heard Mrs Brown calling them inside.

"Coming!" Judy shouted as she scrambled out of the tree house, following her brother.

Paddington hurried after them, but he forgot his hat!

Inside, Mrs Brown was having a clear-out.

"You can't throw these away!"

said Mr Brown, holding up his old snowshoes.

"You can keep them if you promise that you'll wear them," said Mrs Brown.

"I will," said Mr Brown.

The next morning Paddington woke up feeling anxious.

"I left the hat from Aunt Lucy in the tree house," he told Mrs Brown.

"You can get it after breakfast," she said. "Though you'll see the garden looks a little different this morning . . ."

"WOWWW!"

gasped Paddington, looking out of the window at the beautiful snowy scene. He had never seen snow settle before. "It looks like someone has rubbed out the garden!"

After breakfast, Mrs Brown told Jonathan and Judy that Paddington needed them both for a hat-rescue expedition.

"Ready and raring to go on a snowy adventure!" said Jonathan, saluting.

"Just like Captain Scott!" added Judy.

Captain Judy, Jonathan and Paddington trudged through the heavy snow towards the tree house. Their mission: to rescue Paddington's precious hat!

"There it is!" cried Paddington.

Up in the tree house, Paddington was about to pick up his hat, when . . .

TWEET, TWEET! TWEET!

A little robin flew away with it!

"Quick! Follow that hat!" called Paddington, racing after the robin through the house and on to the s l i p p e r y pavement.

"WHOOOAAA!"

Luckily, Judy had just the thing to help – a sledge! They hopped on and zoomed along the icy pavement after the little bird.

"WOOHOO!"

Just as Paddington was about to grab the hat . . .

BUMP!

The sledge hit a lamp post and they all flew off on to the slippery path . . .

WHEEEEEEE!

And slid all the way to the entrance of the park.

"Look at those yeti-sized footprints!" gasped Jonathan.

"Yetis *aren't* real," said Judy. "Come on. We need to get Paddington's hat back!"

They hurried into the park, following the bird, the hat *and* the giant footprints.

As they gazed in wonder at the snow-covered park, Jonathan got smacked by a snowball.

PFFFF! "Oi!" he cried in surprise.

“Looks like Mateo wants a snowball fight!” said Judy, diving behind a tree.

“Ha ha!” giggled Mateo, taking aim again.

Paddington had never had a snowball fight before and didn't know what to do! He tried to throw a snowball, but instead it rolled down the slope, getting bigger

and bigger.

"Oh dear!" he said as the enormous snowball headed straight for Mateo.

It crashed into the tree Mateo was hiding behind and the snow in its branches covered him . . .

SPLAT!

"Oops! Sorry, Mateo!" called Paddington.

"I'm okay!" said Mateo, popping out of the snow.

Suddenly, there was a tweeting noise. **TWEET! TWEET!**

"Look! There's my hat!" Paddington cried, seeing the robin fly up to its nest. Paddington quickly climbed up the tree.

"Hello! Could I have my hat back?" Paddington asked the bird. "Aunt Lucy sent it to me and it's ever so precious."

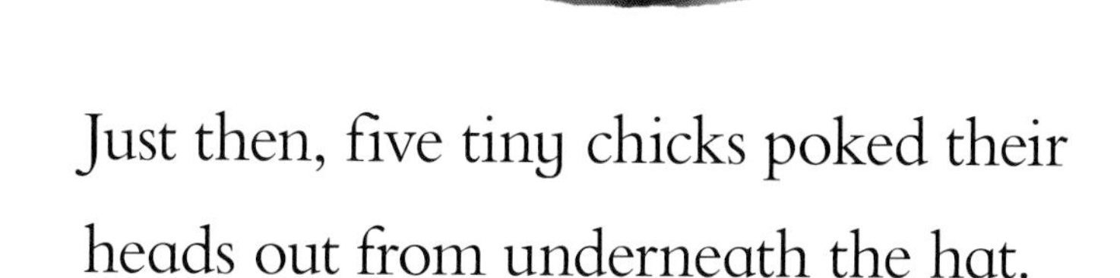

Just then, five tiny chicks poked their heads out from underneath the hat.

POP! POP! POP! POP! POP!

TWEET! TWEET! TWEET! TWEET! TWEET!

"Oh my, how wonderful," whispered Paddington.

“Where’s your hat?” asked Judy when Paddington reached the ground.

“I gave it to the bird,” explained Paddington, pointing up at the nest. “She needs it more than I do to keep her chicks warm.”

Suddenly there was a strange noise . . . **CRRRUNNNCH!**

"Huh! What was that?" asked Judy.

"Look!' gasped Jonathan. "Yeti-sized footprints! It's following us!"

CRRRUNNNCH!

They hid behind a tree and the sound got louder and LOUDER, until . . .

"Hello, everyone!" said Mr Brown.

"AHHHHHH!"

they all screamed.

"DAD?" said Jonathan. "We thought you were a yeti!" Paddington pointed at the massive footprints.

"Oh, that's these snowshoes," said Mr Brown, laughing. "I promised Mrs Brown I'd use them. Come on, everybody. Let's all go home!"

So that's why I don't have your wonderful hat any more, Aunt Lucy. I was able to give a cosy home to a family who really needed it. Somehow, I thought you wouldn't mind.

Love from,

Paddington

P.S. I hope you enjoy this snowball!